W9-CKM-009

We're Counting On You, Grover!

By Michaela Muntean
Illustrated by Joe Ewers

A SESAME STREET/GOLDEN PRESS BOOK

Published by Western Publishing Company, Inc., in conjunction with Children's Television Workshop.

© 1991 Children's Television Workshop. Sesame Street puppet characters © 1991 Jim Henson Productions, Inc. All rights reserved. Printed in the U.S.A. No part of this book may be reproduced or copied in any form without written permission from the publisher. Sesame Street®, the Sesame Street sign®, and A GROWING-UP BOOK are trademarks and service marks of Children's Television Workshop. All other trademarks are the property of Western Publishing Company, Inc. Library of Congress Catalog Card Number: 90-84089   ISBN: 0-307-12050-3/ISBN: 0-307-62250-9 (lib. bdg.)   A MCMXCI

"**T**oday is the day of our play,
Jack and the Beanstalk," announced
Prairie Dawn. "We have to get ready."
   "Oh, may I help?" asked Grover.
"I am a good helper."
   "Thanks, Grover," said Prairie Dawn.
"Let's check our list:
   "A Jack costume for Ernie?"
   "Check," said Ernie.
   "A giant costume for Herry?"
   "Check," said Herry Monster.
   "A mother costume for Bert?"
   "Check," said Bert.
   "A cow costume for Telly?"
   "Moo," said Telly.

Prairie Dawn checked her list again. "Oh, no," she said. "I forgot the beanstalk! We can't have *Jack and the Beanstalk* without the beanstalk. What are we going to do?"

"I have a terrific idea!" said Grover. "We could draw a beanstalk on a long, tall piece of paper and hang it on the wall."

"That's a good idea, Grover," said Prairie Dawn, "but we don't have a long, tall piece of paper."

"I know where we can get one. Mr. Burger, the butcher, has rolls of long paper," said Grover. "I will go ask him for some."

"OK," said Prairie Dawn, "but hurry! The curtain goes up at eight o'clock. We're counting on you, Grover!"

"Do not worry, Prairie Dawn. Faster than a speeding sandwich, I will be back with the longest, tallest piece of paper on Sesame Street!" said Grover.

And he raced out the door and down the street.

Grover had gone only a block when he met Alice,
Big Bird, and Snuffy.

"Hello, Grover," said Big Bird. "Mr. Snuffleupagus and
I are teaching Alice how to jump rope. Would you like
to help us?"

"I would like to," said Grover, "but I am in a big
hurry."

"This will only take a minute," said Big Bird. "We need
someone to turn the other end of the rope so I can
show Alice how to jump."

"All right," said Grover. "But only for a minute."

It took much longer than a minute for Alice to learn how to jump rope, but she finally got the hang of it.

"Thank you, Grover," said Big Bird. "You were a big help."

"No problem," said Grover, but he knew there *would* be a problem if he did not hurry. He had to get to the butcher shop to get that long, tall piece of paper for Prairie Dawn.

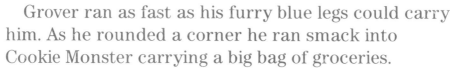

Grover ran as fast as his furry blue legs could carry him. As he rounded a corner he ran smack into Cookie Monster carrying a big bag of groceries.

"Oh, my goodness!" cried Grover. "I am so sorry!"

"Me sorry, too," said Cookie Monster as he watched his oranges roll down the sidewalk. A can of beans rolled into the gutter and a bag of cookies lay at his feet.

"Do not worry, I will pick everything up," said Grover. "But I am afraid your cookies are crunched."

"No matter," said Cookie Monster. "Cookie crumbs just as good as cookies."

Grover scurried after the oranges and picked up the
can of beans from the gutter.

"This bag is torn," said Cookie Monster. "How me
carry home groceries?"

"Do not worry. I, Grover, will help you carry your
groceries home," he said.

And so Grover walked home with Cookie Monster.

Back on Sesame Street, Grover saw a crowd
gathered on the sidewalk.
"I will just take one quick look," he thought.

"Oh, my goodness!" cried Grover. "A juggler.
A juggler juggling is one of my favorite things in the
whole world!"

So Grover stopped to watch. The juggler tossed all
the balls up in the air and caught them again and
again. The juggler didn't drop a single one. Then the
juggler took a bow, and everyone cheered and clapped.
Grover cheered and clapped the loudest.

"Now," said the juggler, "would anyone in the
audience like to try juggling?"

"I would!" cried Grover.

So the juggler handed him the balls and showed him how to toss them up one at a time. The first few times Grover dropped the balls.

"Don't worry," the juggler said. "Juggling takes a lot of practice. Try again."

So Grover tried and tried, and he finally juggled two balls at once without dropping them.

"Yay!" cheered the crowd.

Grover took a bow.

Just then Grover heard someone call his name.

"Over here, Grover," cried Elmo from the steps of
123 Sesame Street.

"Look at my new game. It is called jacks. Will you
please play with me?"

"Jacks?" cried Grover. "Jacks. *Jack and the Beanstalk.*
Beanstalk. Paper. Oh, my goodness! I will play with you
all day tomorrow, Elmo. But not now. I cannot stop
for anything. Good-bye!"

"Good-bye," called Elmo as he watched Grover
race away.

Grover ran the three blocks to the butcher's shop. When he reached the door, he pulled on the handle, but nothing happened.

"It is locked!" gasped Grover. Then he read the sign on the door.

"Closed. Oh, no!" he cried. "I need a long, tall piece of paper that is inside this store. And I am *outside* this store with a big CLOSED sign on the door!" He peered sadly through the window, but Mr. Burger had gone home.

"Sometimes it is not easy being a helpful monster," Grover said with a sigh. "Now what am I going to do?"

There was nothing to do but run back to the school.
This time Grover did not stop for anything. He did not
stop to help. He did not stop to play. He did not stop to
watch, and he was careful not to run into anyone when
he ran around corners.

Finally Grover pushed open the door of the auditorium.

"Jack, you foolish boy, how could you sell our cow for three beans?" he heard Bert say.

As Bert tossed the beans aside Grover tiptoed in. Then he crept behind the stage, where Prairie Dawn was watching the play.

"What happened, Grover?" Prairie asked when she saw him. "We waited and waited for you."

"Oh, so many things happened," Grover said, panting. "First I helped Big Bird turn the jump rope, then I ran into Cookie Monster, and then I stopped to watch a juggler," Grover said. "When I finally got to the butcher's shop, it was closed."

"But we were counting on you," said Prairie Dawn.

"Oh, I am so sorry that I did not get that long, tall piece of paper. Now there is no beanstalk for the play," Grover cried.

"Take a look," said Prairie Dawn.

Grover peeked out onto the stage and saw—a beanstalk. The leaves were painted on many little pieces of paper taped and stapled and stuck together.

"It's not as good a beanstalk as it would have been with one long, tall piece of paper," said Prairie Dawn. "But the show must go on!"

Grover was quiet for a moment. "I let everybody down," he said. "I am sorry."

"I know you are," said Prairie Dawn.

"Will you ever let me help with a play again?" Grover asked.

"Of course," said Prairie Dawn. "Our next production is *Goldilocks and the Three Bears*. You can be in charge of the bowls of porridge."

"Oh, thank you, Prairie Dawn!" said Grover. "I will get you a hundred bowls. I will get you a million bowls!"

"Three will be enough," said Prairie Dawn.

"All right," said Grover. "I will get one big bowl, one medium-sized bowl, and one baby bowl. This is one monster you can count on from now on!"